Lin-Lin and The Gulls

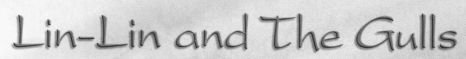

Written by Laura Appleton-Smith

Illustrated by Carol Vredenburgh

Laura Appleton-Smith holds a degree in English from Middlebury College.
Laura is a primary schoolteacher who has combined her talents in creative writing with
her experience in early childhood education to create *Books to Remember*.
She lives in New Hampshire with her husband Terry.

Carol Vredenburgh graduated Summa Cum Laude from Syracuse University and has worked
as an artist and illustrator ever since. This is the fourth book she has illustrated for Flyleaf Publishing.

A Book to Remember™
Published by Flyleaf Publishing
Post Office Box 287, Lyme, NH 03768

For orders or information, contact us at **(800) 449-7006**.
Please visit our website at **www.flyleafpublishing.com**

First Edition
Library of Congress Catalog Card Number: 2002090759
Hard cover ISBN: 1-929262-05-1
Soft cover ISBN: 1-929262-06-x

*This story is adapted from an ancient Chinese myth of the Liezi.
The actual myth is printed at the end of this book.*

For Terry

LAS

For Isabella, a beautiful free spirit.

CV

Lin-Lin lived in a hut next to the sea.

Lin-Lin loved seagulls.

At sunset, Lin-Lin went to the spot
where the land met the sea.

Standing in the sunlit swells,
Lin-Lin beckoned the gulls
and the gulls flocked to her.

If Lin-Lin ran, the gulls
flapped their wings
next to her.

If Lin-Lin swam, the gulls
bobbed on the swells
next to her.

If Lin-Lin sat on the sand,
the gulls nested
next to her.

As the sun dropped past the tranquil sea,
Lin-Lin was filled with
gladness.

Often, on the trip back to her hut,
Lin-Lin stopped to visit the old woman.

The old woman's legs were bent and stiff.
She could not travel to the spot where
the land met the sea.

The old woman asked Lin-Lin to tell her
of the sea
and the gulls
and the sunset.

Lin-Lin was glad to tell the old woman.

On one visit, the old woman asked Lin-Lin
to bring her six gulls.

"Trap the gulls in this basket.
They can dwell in this hut.
Then I will be glad."

On the trip back to her hut Lin-Lin was distressed.

The blustering wind gusted past her.

Lin-Lin wanted the old woman to fill herself
with gladness...

But Lin-Lin felt that the spirit of the gulls
would be lost if they lived in a hut and had
no sea,
no sun,
no wind,
and no sand.

That night Lin-Lin was restless.
She tossed in her bed.
It was as if the tumult of the wind
was gusting in her.

At last, Lin-Lin resolved that she must
bring a basket of gulls to the old woman.

The next sunset,
Lin-Lin had the basket
in her hands
when she went
to the sea.

She was filled with sadness.

But when she got to the spot
where the land met the sea,
not a gull was there.

And for this,
Lin-Lin was glad.

A man who lived by the sea loved seagulls.
Every morning at daybreak he would go to the seaside and play with the gulls.
Hundreds of gulls would come to him and not fly away.

His father said, "I heard that seagulls like to play with you.
Catch a few for me so that I can play with them too."

The next morning when he went to the seaside
the seagulls swooped about in the skies but none came down to him.

Liezi

Lin-Lin and The Gulls is decodable with the 26 phonetic alphabet sounds, and the ability to blend those sounds together.

Puzzle Words are words used in the story that are either irregular or may have sound/spelling correspondences that the reader may not be familiar with.

The **Puzzle Word Review List** contains Puzzle Words that have been introduced in in previous books in the *Books to Remember* Series.

Please Note: If all of the words on this page are pre-taught and the reader knows the 26 phonetic alphabet sounds, plus the phonograms listed above, and has the ability to blend those sounds together, this book is 100% phonetically decodable.

Puzzle Words:
sea
seagulls
old
visit
woman

Puzzle Word Review List:	
a	that
as	the
be	their
could	then
for	there
her	they
herself	this
I	to
night	wanted
no	was
of	were
one	when
she	where
	with
	would

"ed" words:
ask**ed**
beckon**ed**
bobb**ed**
distress**ed**
dropp**ed**
fill**ed**
flapp**ed**
flock**ed**
gust**ed**
liv**ed**
lov**ed**
nest**ed**
resolv**ed**
stopp**ed**
toss**ed**
want**ed**